STORIES FROM

Alaska

Folklore of the World

Each of the Folklore of the World Books contains carefully selected myths and folktales most representative of a single country. These books will help children to understand people in other lands and will help them to develop an appreciation for their customs and culture. Peace for the world can come only through the spreading of this understanding and appreciation.

The Folklore Books are the third step in the Dolch program, *Steps to a Lifetime Reading Habit*. The series on these graded steps, starting with the most elementary, are: the First Reading Books, the Basic Vocabulary Books, the Folklore Books, and the Pleasure Reading Books.

These Folklore Books are written almost entirely in the Storyteller's Vocabulary, a list of 684 words found by research to be the most useful words in telling stories to young people. This list fits in between that of the Basic Vocabulary Books and that of the Pleasure Reading Books.

Folklore Books are prepared under the direction of Edward W. Dolch, Professor of Education, Emeritus, University of Illinois. In all the series, emphasis is placed on good storytelling and literary quality, as well as on simplicity of vocabulary.

Books in this series are: (to date)

Stories from Alaska
Stories from India
Stories from Italy
Stories from Hawaii
Stories from Mexico
Stories from Spain
Stories from Japan

STORIES FROM

Alaska

Folklore of the World

by EDWARD W. DOLCH
and MARGUERITE P. DOLCH

illustrated by
CARL HELDT

GARRARD PUBLISHING COMPANY
CHAMPAIGN, ILLINOIS

Foreword

Ever since 1867, when the land we now call Alaska was purchased by the United States, we have been gradually becoming acquainted with the resources of this vast country. We have been learning, among other things, about the various peoples who are native to Alaska. These native tribes fall into two divisions, the Indians and the Eskimo. The Eskimo have lived for a very long time in the North and West of Alaska, along the ocean where they get their living. The Indians have lived in the interior, along the southern coast, and on the long narrow strip that extends down toward the rest of the United States.

Both Indians and Eskimo have folklore that is of great interest, both as stories and also as showing the life and thinking of these peoples. From the many stories that are recorded, we have selected a number which show a great deal about the Indians and the Eskimo as they were until they began to imitate the white settlers. These stories naturally reflect the hard life that these people lived, as well as the natural conditions that surrounded them.

If these stories from the folklore of the Forty-ninth State are of interest, the reader will wish to go to the other volumes of Indian and Eskimo folklore from Alaska.

E. W. DOLCH

Santa Barbara, California

Contents

Raven Gets Light

Raven lived in the beginning of the world. Then there was very little light. In the sky, there was no Sun or Moon or Stars. There was very little light to go fishing. More than all other things, the people needed light. Raven wanted to help the people get light.

Far up on the Nass River, there lived a mighty Chief. Raven heard that the Chief had three beautiful boxes. In one box he kept the Stars. In another box he kept the Moon. And in the biggest box he kept the Sun.

Raven said to himself,

"My people must have light. This is a thing that I must do."

Now Raven could change himself into anything that he wanted to be. So he changed himself into the baby grandson of the Chief.

The Chief loved his grandson very much. He gave him everything that he wanted. One day the baby grandson began to cry. He cried and cried and cried. He pointed to the three boxes.

The mighty Chief was afraid that his grandson would get sick. So he gave to the baby the box in which there were the Stars.

"You may play with the box," said the Chief. "But be sure that you do not open the box."

The baby grandson played with the box on the floor. Then, when no one was looking, Raven opened the box, and the Stars went right up through the smoke hole in the lodge. All the people on earth saw the Stars. They said, "How beautiful."

The Chief was very sad to have lost his Stars. But he loved his grandson and did not scold him.

Raven did not think that the Stars gave enough light.

One day the baby grandson began

to cry again. He cried and cried. He kept pointing to the two boxes that held the Moon and the Sun.

The grandfather said,

"I will have to give my grandson the box that has the Moon in it. He will not stop crying." So the Grandfather gave his grandson the box with the Moon in it.

Raven took the Moon out of the box. It was round like a ball. He sat on the floor beside his mother and played with the Moon. But when no one was looking, Raven threw the Moon out of the smoke hole in the top of the lodge. The Moon went right up into the

sky. The people on earth saw
the Moon and said, "Oh, how
beautiful."

"You have lost two of my
greatest treasures," said the
grandfather. "But do not cry."

But Raven said to himself,

"The people on earth must have
the Sun. This is the thing that I
must do for them. And the Sun
is still in the big box."

After a time, the baby grandson
began to cry again. His mother
could not stop his crying.

The servants said to the mother,

"Your baby is sick. His face is
red, and his eyes are rolling in

his head. His arms and legs are stiff."

The mother began to cry. She said to her father, the great Chief,

"My baby will not stop crying. He will die. He keeps pointing to that big box. Let him have it, for what good will your treasures be if your grandson dies?"

"My grandson must not die," said the Chief.

The Chief had his servants give the big box where the Sun was hidden to his grandson.

"Do not open the box or what is in it will hurt your eyes very much," said the Chief.

The baby laughed and laughed. He played with the big box. The servants watched him very carefully. But one day the servants were busy. The baby, with a glad cry that sounded like the call of the Raven, took the box in his arms. He changed his shape into that of a raven and flew up to the smoke hole of the lodge, carrying the box with him.

The mighty Chief saw what was happening. By his magic he tried to make the smoke hole too small for the Raven to get through. But the Raven pushed through the smoke hole, which was all black

from the smoke of many fires.
And that is why a raven is
always black.

So the Raven got through the
smoke hole with the box that held
the Sun. The box was very heavy.
He changed himself into a strong
man, and then he carried the big
box down to the people who lived
at the mouth of the Nass River.

By now, Raven was very hungry.
He asked the people for fish to
eat. But the people said,

"Go and catch your own fish."

This made Raven very angry.
He opened the box and Sun came
out with a noise like thunder. The

people were very much afraid. Some ran to the sea. Some ran to the mountains. And some ran up the River Nass. That is why, wherever you go, you will find people that belong to the Raven.

But the Sun went up into the sky, and now there was light in the world.

The Two Friends

The son of the Chief had a very good friend. The two boys played together all the time. And they were always trying to see who could make the most arrows.

One time they had made a lot of arrows. The Chief's son said,

"Let us go up to the hill back of our village. Let us see how far we can shoot our arrows."

The two boys went up to the hill just as the Moon was coming up.

"Look at the Moon," said the friend. "It looks just like my mother's cooking pot."

"Do not speak that way about the Moon," said the Chief's son. "The Moon will be angry with you."

Suddenly the Moon became dark, and there was a ring of light around the boys.

When the Moon became bright again, and the ring of light was gone, the Chief's son could not find his friend. He called and he called, but his friend did not answer.

"My friend must have run up the hill to get away from the light," said the Chief's son to himself.

The Chief's son ran up the hill. But he could not find his friend.

The boy sat down on the hill. He did not know what to do. He was sure that the Moon had taken his friend into the sky.

All about the boy were the many arrows that he and his friend had made. As he sat there thinking, he took up his bow and put an arrow to it. He saw a star very close to the Moon. He aimed at that star and shot the arrow.

The boy waited to see where the arrow would fall. But it did not fall. He shot another arrow. But it did not come back to earth. The Chief's son shot all the arrows at the star, and not one of them came back to earth.

The boy sat on the hill in the light of the Moon. He wondered where the arrows had gone. Soon he was very tired. He lay back and went to sleep.

When the boy woke up, it was morning. He looked up into the sky. There he saw a ladder made of arrows, coming down to him from the sky.

The Chief's son began to climb the ladder of arrows. He climbed and he climbed. All day he climbed. When night came, he was very tired. He went to sleep, holding on to the ladder of arrows.

The next morning, the boy started to climb again. He climbed and he climbed. At last he reached the top, and he found himself in the Land of the Sky. Here he saw a beautiful lake. He was so tired that he lay down beside the lake and fell asleep.

The Chief's son thought he was dreaming, for he thought he heard someone say,

"Get up. I have come for you."

The Chief's son opened his eyes and saw a girl standing before him.

"Get up," said the girl. "My grandmother has sent me to bring you to our house."

The girl took the Chief's son to a little house where an old woman lived.

"Why did you come up here?" asked the old woman, who was called the Sky Woman.

"I came to find my friend," said the Chief's son.

"He is in the house of the

Moon," said the Sky Woman. "I often hear him crying."

The old woman gave the boy some food. Then she said, "I will help you so that you can find your friend."

Back from the Moon

The Chief's son had climbed a ladder of arrows up to the Sky Country. He wanted to find his friend, who had been taken by the Moon. In the Sky Country, he found the Sky Woman.

The Sky Woman gave the boy a large cone from a pine tree. She gave him a wild rose bush. And she gave him a stone.

"The Moon tries to keep anyone that comes to his house. But these will help you to get away from the Moon," said the Sky Woman.

Then the Chief's son went to

the Moon's house. He heard his friend crying. He climbed up on the roof of the Moon's house. He looked down through the smoke hole into the house.

There, on a shelf near the smoke hole, was his friend. His friend was crying.

The Chief's son called to his friend, and the other boy looked up. Then the Chief's son said,

"See this big pine cone I have. Put this big pine cone on the shelf that you are on, and climb up the cone to the smoke hole. Then we will both run away together."

The friend did just as he was

told. He got out of the smoke hole, and the two boys jumped to the ground and started to run.

When the crying stopped, the people in the house had looked up. The friend had just got through the smoke hole, and the people saw only the big pine cone.

The Moon saw what had happened. He ran out of the house and started after the boys.

The boys had a head start, but the Moon got nearer and nearer. So the Chief's son threw the rose bush over his shoulder. All at once the rose bush grew and grew right in the way of the Moon.

The Moon had a hard time getting through the rose bush. Then he started after the boys.

Then the Chief's son threw the stone over his shoulder. All at once the stone became a great stone mountain. And the Moon could not get over the mountain.

At last the boys got to the Sky Woman's house. She gave them something to eat. Then she said,

"Go and lie down beside the lake. Think hard of the hill where you played together. Then go to sleep and you will wake up on the hill."

The boys went to the lake. But the Chief's son kept thinking of the Sky Woman and how she had helped him. Before he knew it, both of the boys were back in the Sky Woman's house.

"You did not do as I told you," said the Sky Woman. "Go back to the lake and think only of the hill where you used to play."

The boys went back to the lake. This time they thought only of the hill where they used to play. They went to sleep, and when they woke up they were on the hill back of their village.

The boys heard a drum beating in the village. From the sound, they knew that the people were dancing the death dance.

The boys went down to the woods near the village and watched the death dance. The people had cut their hair and had painted their faces black. The people danced and feasted all day and far into the night.

In the morning, the Chief's son saw his younger brother come out of the Great House. He said,

"Go and tell our father that I am not dead. I have come back from the Moon."

The little boy was afraid, but he went to his mother and said,

"I have seen my brother and his friend. They have come back from the Moon."

The mother was very angry.

"Do not talk like that," she said. "Your brother and his friend are dead."

But the little boy kept crying. The mother went out. She saw her son and his friend.

Then all the people of the village came again to the Great House. There was feasting and dancing. But the dance was not the dance of death.

Beaver and Porcupine

A long time ago, Beaver and Porcupine were friends. Bear was not their friend. He tried to catch Beaver so that he might eat him. But Bear was afraid of Porcupine, for Porcupine's pointed quills could hurt him.

Beaver knew how to build a warm, dry house in the middle of a lake. In those days, Porcupine liked to sleep in Beaver's house.

One day, Beaver saw that the water was going down in the lake where he had made his house. He

knew that Bear must have broken
the dam that Beaver had made
to keep the water in the lake. He
told Porcupine, and Porcupine
went out to look around.

"It is just as you thought,"
said Porcupine, when he came
back. "Bear has broken the dam
that made your lake. Now he will
want to get into your house and
eat you. But do not be afraid.
Bear will not hurt you as long as
I am in your house."

Then Porcupine went to sleep
in Beaver's house. After a time,
Porcupine woke up and said,

"I am hungry. I must go out and climb a tree to get some young leaves to eat."

"Oh, do not leave me alone," said Beaver. "I am afraid that Bear will eat me."

"I will take you with me," said Porcupine. "Climb on my back and I will take you up the tree so that Bear cannot get you."

So Porcupine took Beaver to the top of a tree. Then Porcupine began to eat green leaves. He went from one place to another to find green leaves. Pretty soon, Porcupine had enough green leaves.

He went off and forgot all about Beaver up in the tree. And Beaver could not climb down from the tree.

Beaver did not know what to do. He called and called, but Porcupine did not hear him. At last Squirrel, who was Beaver's friend, came and showed him how to get down from the tree.

Bear had gone away. So Beaver and his friends fixed the dam. Soon there was much water in the lake around Beaver's house.

The next time Porcupine came to sleep in Beaver's house, Beaver said,

"Come and swim with me in the lake."

"I cannot swim," said Porcupine.

"I will carry you on my back," said Beaver. "You will enjoy a swim in the lake."

Porcupine got on Beaver's back. And Beaver swam with him to the middle of the lake where an old stump stuck out of the water.

"Get on the stump," said Beaver. "I want to rest awhile."

As soon as Porcupine had climbed up on the stump, Beaver swam away.

"Come back. Come back," cried Porcupine. "I cannot swim."

But Beaver was thinking of how Porcupine had left him in the top of the tree. He did not go back to get Porcupine off the stump.

Porcupine did not know how to get away from the stump. He could not swim. So Porcupine cried and cried. At last he began to sing a song.

North Wind, North Wind.

Let it become frozen.

Let it become frozen.

North Wind, North Wind.

Come and help me.

The North Wind heard the Porcupine sing. The North Wind

blew and blew. The lake became frozen. Porcupine walked across the ice and went to his own home.

Porcupine has never been a friend of Beaver from that day to this.

The Fat in the Box

A Chief lived in a big house in the middle of a large village. The Chief liked to ask other tribes to come and eat at his house, for he was a great Chief.

The wife of the Chief, and all the servants, were kept busy keeping the fat boxes full, so that there would always be enough for a feast for the guests.

One day the big daughter and the little daughter of the Chief were hungry. They ate some fat from one of the boxes. The mother saw them and was very angry.

"Shame on you, my daughters," said the mother. "You know that you are never to eat between meals, and that you must never eat the fat from the boxes which your father keeps for his guests."

The mother was so angry that she slapped the big daughter's cheeks. She said to the little daughter,

"You are too little to know better. I will not slap your cheeks. But never eat between meals again."

The older daughter was very

proud. She did not cry when her mother slapped her cheeks.

"You like to eat so much," said the mother. "You had better marry the Mountain Man. He is the greatest hunter in the world. His wife will always have the fat from the mountain sheep to eat."

That night, when everyone in the great house was sleeping, the girl and her little sister went out of the house. They went to the mountains to find the Mountain Man.

The next morning the mother called her daughters.

"It is time to get up."

When she found that her daughters were not in the house, she went up and down the village calling to them. But no one had seen her daughters.

Then the people of the village went out to hunt for the girls. They hunted all day long. The girls heard the people calling to them. They hid in the woods. The people did not find them.

The people of the big village believed that a great bear had killed the daughters of the Chief. After many days the Chief held a death dance for his daughters.

The Chief asked the tribe of the mother to come to the dance. He asked all the people of his own tribe. The Chief was going to give a potlatch feast.

A potlatch feast was one at which gifts were given away. Sometimes a Chief gave away all that he had at a potlatch. It left him very poor, but everyone thought him a great man.

Whenever anyone at a potlatch feast was given a gift, he had to give back, within a year, a gift that was better than the one that had been given him.

A potlatch feast was often given for those who had died. When fat was burned in the fire, and when blankets were given away, it meant that those who had died would not be hungry or cold.

At this potlatch feast, the Chief and the mother's brothers danced the death dance. They all wore their dancing robes, and their wooden hats, which were carved to look like animals. The women sang and beat the drums. They all thought that the death dance made those who had died very happy.

But the mother of the girls was very sad, for she had slapped the older daughter's cheeks for eating between meals. She knew that was why the daughters had run away from their home.

The Mountain Man

The two girls who had run away
from home went through the
woods. They ate the berries that
they found. They drank the water
from the little streams. They
walked and walked.

They began to climb up the
mountains. Now they were cold
and hungry. The little girl was
crying. She wanted her big sister
to take her home. But the big
sister said,

"Do not cry, little one. We will
find the Mountain Man and he
will take care of us."

Soon the sisters heard someone chopping wood. They looked
through the trees and saw a big
man chopping down a tree. He
was the biggest man the girls had
ever seen. And his face was painted
red. The girls knew at once that
this was the Mountain Man. They
went toward him.

The Mountain Man looked up
and saw the two girls.

"What are you doing up on the
mountain?" asked the Mountain
Man. "You look tired and hungry."

"My mother slapped my cheeks,"
said the older girl. "That is why
I left home."

"We were hungry and we ate some of the fat out of the boxes," said the little girl. "And I am hungry now." She began to cry. She was tired and very hungry.

"Come," said the Mountain Man. "I will take you to my house. I have lots of food, and you shall have all the fat you want to eat."

The Mountain Man lived in a fine house. There was an old woman who looked after the house. The Mountain Man called her "Grandmother."

"Grandmother," said the Mountain Man. "Go to the smoke

house and get a mountain sheep
that is good and fat. Roast it by
the fire and give the girls something to eat, for they are tired
and hungry."

The old woman was very cross.
But she gave the girls something
to eat. The Mountain Man put
some wood on the fire in the
middle of the house. Soon the
girls were warm and happy. They
talked with the Mountain Man.

The older sister was very
beautiful. The Mountain Man said
to her,

"Will you stay with me and be
my wife?"

"Yes," said the girl. "My mother said that I should marry the Mountain Man, for he was the best hunter in the world."

One day the Mountain Man went out to hunt in the mountains. But before he left the house, he said to his wife,

"The old woman may try to harm you and your sister while I am away. I will leave you this big stick. Be careful, for she does not like anyone to stay in my house."

The young wife and her little sister sat by the fire. But the wife had a big stick by her side. She watched everything that the old woman did.

First the old woman put a lot of wood on the fire. The smoke went out of the smoke hole in the top of the house. Then the old woman went to the smoke house. She came back into the house with a fat mountain sheep. She put this in the middle of the fire. The fat on the mountain sheep began to burn.

The old woman was going to push the burning mountain sheep over on to the young wife in order to kill her. Before she could do it, the young wife took her big stick and pushed the burning sheep over on the old woman. The old woman was burned up in the fire. And that was the end of the old woman.

The Magic Basket

When the Mountain Man came home, he said to his wife,

"Where is the old woman?"

"She was going to kill me by pushing a burning mountain sheep over on me," said the wife. "I took the big stick which you had given me and pushed the burning mountain sheep on to her. The old woman was burned up in the fire."

"I am glad the old woman did not kill you," said the Mountain Man. "You are a good wife."

The Mountain Man and his wife
and her little sister lived in the
big house on the mountain. They
were very happy, and there was
always the fat of the mountain
sheep to eat.

One day, the Mountain Man
said to his wife,

"It is time you took your little
sister back to her mother."

"Yes, yes," said the little sister,
"I want to see my mother and
my little brothers."

"Make a little basket no bigger
than your thumb," said the
Mountain Man to his wife. "When

you have made the basket, I will show you my magic."

The wife worked and worked to make a little basket no bigger than her thumb. The first basket she made was as big as her head. The second basket she made was as big as her hand. But the third basket she made was no bigger than her thumb. That was what the husband wanted.

The Mountain Man took the little basket to the smoke house where he kept his meat. He shook the little basket and it became a big, big basket. The Mountain

Man filled the basket with meat. Then he shook the basket that was full of meat, and the basket and all that was in it became small again. It could be carried very easily.

Mountain Man and his wife and her little sister started down the mountain. When the girls reached their father's house, their little brother came running out of the door. He ran back into the house to tell his mother.

"Mother! Mother!" he cried, "my sisters have come home."

"Your sisters were killed by a bear," said the mother. "Your father had a death dance for them."

"I know my sisters," cried the little boy. "They are outside the house. There is a big man with them."

Then the mother went out of the house and saw her two daughters. She was so happy she cried. She called the father, who was the Chief of the village. He was happy to see them and to see the Mountain Man.

All the people who lived in the big village came out to the Chief's house. They were glad to see the two daughters. They wanted to see the Mountain Man because they had heard so many stories about him.

The older sister said to her mother,

"Send the servants outside to bring into the house the basket of meat that my husband brings as a present."

Then the Mountain Man shook the little basket that he carried in his hand. It became a big, big basket filled with the smoked meat of the mountain sheep.

The basket was so heavy that the servants could not lift it. But the Mountain Man picked up the basket and carried it into the house.

There was great feasting, for there was so much meat that the people could not eat all of it. After the feasting had lasted for three days and three nights, the Mountain Man and his wife went back to their home in the mountains.

Blackskin

A Chief and all his men wanted to be very strong. They wanted to be strong enough to kill the sea lions.

So every morning, the Chief and all his men ran down to the sea. They jumped into the cold, cold water and bathed.

When they came out of the sea, they tried to twist the village tree around and around. They did all these things so that they would become very, very strong.

The Chief had a nephew who would one day become chief, because in that tribe, the nephew became the chief, and not the Chief's own son. This nephew slept all day. He would not go down to the sea with the Chief and his men and bathe in the cold water.

All the people laughed at the nephew. They thought he was a coward not to bathe in the cold sea. They called him Blackskin to make fun of him. At one time he had slept too near the fire and the smoke had made his face black.

But Blackskin was a good man. He did not fight and he did not lie. He always brought wood for the old women who looked after the fires. He did not care if the people laughed at him.

Blackskin slept all day. But at night, when everybody was sleeping, he went down to the sea. He jumped into the cold, cold water. He was growing stronger all the time. But Blackskin did not want anyone to know how strong he was growing.

One night, when Blackskin was bathing in the sea, he heard a whistle. He saw on the beach a man who wore a bearskin. He had never seen this man before.

"I am called Strength," called the man. "I have come to help you."

When Blackskin went up to the man, Strength lifted him high in the air. Then he threw him down on the sand.

"You are not strong enough," cried Strength. "I will help you, but you must not tell anyone that you saw me."

In the big house of the Chief, the boys often wrestled. The boys would make fun of Blackskin.

They would wrestle with him, and he always let them throw him to the ground. He did not want anyone to know how strong he was.

The men laughed and laughed.

"Blackskin is like a child," they said. "He cannot wrestle even with children."

Blackskin did not say anything when they made fun of him.

One night, when Blackskin was bathing in the sea, he heard Strength whistle again. Blackskin came out of the water and the two men wrestled. Blackskin lifted the other man from the ground.

"Stop," cried Strength. "Do not throw me to the ground. Now you are strong enough."

Blackskin went up the village tree. He twisted it around and around. Then he untwisted it and left it as it was.

The next morning, the Chief and all his men went down to the sea. When they came out of the water, the Chief went up to the tree and twisted it around and around. All of the men saw him do it.

"Look, look," cried all the men. "Our Chief is strong enough to twist the tree. Now we can go out in our canoes and hunt the sea lions."

Blackskin smiled when he heard this. But he did not tell anyone that he had twisted the tree in the night.

The Sea Lion Hunt

All the men were getting ready to hunt the sea lions. The people liked sea lion meat best of all. But the sea lion was very fierce. Only the strongest hunters could kill the sea lions.

Blackskin sat by the fire in the Chief's big house. He watched the smoke going up through the smoke hole in the roof of the house. He did not say anything to anyone.

The men were going by the door. Each wore his best shirt for the sea lion hunt. That was what the hunters always did.

The Chief's wife came up to Blackskin. "Will the men ask you to go on the sea lion hunt?" she said.

"They will not ask me. But I am going," he said. "Bring me a clean shirt."

The Chief's wife brought a clean shirt and a band for his hair. She put these, with some food, in a small bundle. Blackskin put the bundle inside his old shirt and went down to the sea. He went toward the big canoe.

All the people were watching the young men push the big canoe out into the water.

The hunters were ready to go. Blackskin stood and watched them.

When the Chief and his hunters were seated in the canoe, Blackskin walked out into the water.

"I will go with you," he said.

Everybody laughed and shouted,

"Look at Blackskin, the great sea lion hunter. He does not even have a clean shirt."

The young men pushed the big canoe away from the shore. But Blackskin took hold of the canoe and held it, and the men could not move it. They all turned and looked at the Chief.

"Let my nephew come with us," said the Chief. "He can dip the water out of the bottom of the canoe."

The hunters looked at Blackskin and said,

"How many sea lions are you going to kill?"

But Blackskin did not say a word. He got into the canoe. He sat in the bottom of the canoe and went to sleep.

At last the Chief and his hunters came to the island where the sea lions lived. As the canoe came up to the shore, the Chief jumped

out. Sea lions were all around
him.

The Chief caught a small sea
lion by the tail and hit it on the
rocks and killed it. Then he went
after a big sea lion, the biggest
sea lion of them all.

The Chief was a strong man.
He jumped on top of the sea lion.
He was going to twist its head as
he had twisted the tree in the
village. But the sea lion threw him
off. He fell and hit his head on a
rock and was killed.

When the hunters saw what had
happened, they paddled the canoe

out to sea. But Blackskin put on his clean shirt and the band on his hair. He stood up in the front of the canoe and spoke as a chief would speak.

"Take the canoe back to the island of the sea lions. I will kill the sea lion that killed my uncle."

The hunters knew that a chief had spoken. They paddled the canoe back to the island.

Blackskin stepped out of the canoe. He went after the sea lion that had killed his uncle. He twisted the sea lion's head until it was dead. Then he hit many of the smaller sea lions and killed them.

Now the hunters were afraid of Blackskin, for he was very strong. They remembered how they had made fun of him. So the men paddled the canoe away from the island, and left Blackskin alone.

The House of the Sea Lions

Blackskin was alone on the island of the sea lions. Dead sea lions were all about him. He did not know what to do.

Blackskin was very tired. So he lay down and went to sleep. In his sleep he heard the beating of sticks. Suddenly he heard someone say,

"I have come for you."

When Blackskin looked around, he could see no one. Then he heard the call again,

"I have been sent to get you."

Blackskin looked around again. But he saw nothing but a black duck swimming in the water.

Now, as everyone knows, every animal lives in his own place. Fish live in the water, and birds live in the air. The duck can fly in the air but he can also go under the water.

The shaman, or man of magic, had told Blackskin that sometimes a man can change himself into a fish or into a bird, or even into a duck.

"Get on my back," said the duck, "and keep your eyes shut."

Blackskin was not afraid. He went out to the duck. The duck became much larger. Blackskin lay on the back of the duck and shut his eyes. He felt that he was going down, down, down to the bottom of the sea.

"Open your eyes," said the duck.

When Blackskin opened his eyes, he was in a very fine house. It was the house of the sea lions under the sea. Here the sea lions looked just like people.

In the house of the sea lions, lying on a bed, was a boy who was in great pain. He was crying all of the time. Blackskin looked at the boy and saw that there was in his side a bone spear head.

Blackskin cut the bone spear head out of the boy's side He washed the place with clean water. The boy got well at once.

The boy was the son of the Chief of the sea lions. The Chief said to Blackskin,

"You have made my son well. Ask for anything and I shall give it to you."

Blackskin had looked around in the house. He had seen a beautiful box that was hanging overhead.

"I would like that beautiful box," said Blackskin.

"It shall be yours," said the Chief of the sea lions. "But take good care of that box, for it is the most wonderful thing I have. It is a magic box. It is the 'box of the winds.' Call any wind you want, and whistle. The wind you have called will come to the box."

The Chief took down the box and gave it to Blackskin. Blackskin got into the box, for it was a very large one. Suddenly he found himself in the middle of the sea. He called for the wind that would take him back to his own village.

When he whistled, the wind came and blew him and the box. Soon Blackskin saw the shore of his own village. The wind blew the box up on the shore.

All the people were glad to see Blackskin again. The first thing he did was to hang the box up on the tree by the village. He did not want it to be hurt.

The people told Blackskin that he was their new Chief. But some of the young men ran away into the woods. They were afraid of Blackskin. They remembered how they had made fun of him. They remembered how they had gone off and left him on the sea lion island.

But Blackskin was not angry with any of the young men.

"Do not be cruel," he said. "If you are cruel, you will be ashamed of yourself, and others will be ashamed of you. And do not make fun of anyone as you did of me when my uncle was Chief."

Blackskin was a good man. He was a good Chief to his people.

The Lake Monster

A long time ago, the son of a Chief married the daughter of another Chief. The young man went to live in the house of his wife's mother, as the custom was. But the mother-in-law did not like him.

All day long the wife's mother made fun of her son-in-law. She called him a lazy man and said that he did not work like the other men in the village. He did not cut wood. And he did not go fishing.

Now there was a lake up in the mountains that the young man often thought about. He had heard many stories that the old men told about a monster that lived in this lake. The young man wanted to go to the lake and to see this monster.

When summer came, the salmon came up the river by the village. All the people of the village went out to fish for the salmon. The young man went with them. But he caught only two salmon. Then he went away, and no one saw where he went.

The beautiful wife cried for her husband. But her mother said,

"I hope I never see your lazy husband again. They say he caught only two salmon, and then he went away. I am glad he is gone."

But the young man had taken his two salmon and had climbed up to the lake in the mountains. There he had made a fire and smoked the salmon so that they would keep.

The young man made himself a little house beside the lake. Then he took his ax and cut down a

big tree that stood beside the lake.
When the tree fell into the lake,
the young man said,

"Now I shall make a trap to
catch the monster that lives in
the lake."

The young man split the tree
part way down, and kept the two
halves apart with sticks. He put
the tree in the water of the lake
with the two halves held apart,
and with water in between them.

Then the young man put one
of the salmon on his line and let
it down in the lake right between
the halves of the tree. He waited
until he felt a pull on his line.

Then he pulled up the line very quickly. The monster came up to the top, right after the salmon. So the monster was right between the halves of the tree.

Quickly, the young man kicked the sticks that held the halves of the tree apart. The halves came together and caught the head of the monster. He made a great noise in the water, but soon he was dead.

The young man used his sticks to separate the two halves of the tree. Then he took the monster out of the water and skinned it. He dried the skin very carefully.

Now the old men had said that if a man could crawl into the skin of the lake monster, he could go down under the water. So the young man crawled into the skin of the monster and swam down under the water. There he found a beautiful house where the monster had lived.

At last the young man came up from the bottom of the lake. He crawled out of the skin of the monster. When the skin was dry, he put it into a hollow tree where nothing would hurt it. Then the young man went back to the village.

The beautiful wife was very glad to see her husband. But the mother-in-law said,

"I hoped that I would never see that lazy man again. But now he has come back to eat the salmon that the rest of us have caught."

For a time, there was plenty of salmon. All the people in the village had all they wanted to eat. But soon all the dried salmon was gone. The men went out but they could not catch any fish. The people in the village were hungry.

The Young Man Helps

The people in the village were hungry. The dried salmon was all gone. And the men could not catch any more fish.

One day the young man said to his wife,

"I am going away. Every night I shall be gone. I will return in the morning. But if I am not home before the raven calls, you will know that I am dead."

The young man went up to the lake in the mountains and got the monster's skin out of the hollow tree. He put it on and went down into the lake. He swam from the lake down into the river by the village and then out into the sea. He swam around in the sea and found a big salmon.

It was dark as he brought the salmon to the shore by the village. He put it in front of his mother-in-law's house. Then he carried the skin back to the lake and hid it in the hollow tree. He got back to his wife before the raven called.

In the morning, the mother-in-law found the big salmon before her house. She called the Chief, her husband, and said,

"Look what my spirits have brought to me. Go and call the people of the village."

The young man slept all day. In the evening, he left and was gone all night. But he was home again before the raven called.

In the morning, the mother-in-law found two big salmon before her house. The young man whispered to his wife that it was he who had caught the salmon.

"But do not tell anyone what I have told you," he said.

Then the young man went to sleep and slept all day. The mother-in-law was very angry with

him and called him Sleep Fellow.
But the wife only smiled.

Now the mother-in-law began to
be very proud of herself. She
began to think that she was a
shaman and could have anything
that she wished. She wished for
a halibut, which is a fish larger
than a salmon.

The next morning, a large
halibut was in front of the mother-
in-law's house. Now the woman
was sure that she was a shaman.

The Chief had a dancing apron
like the shamen wear made for his
wife. He had rattles made and a
mask carved like an animal.

The mother-in-law danced and shook her rattles. Then she asked the Food Spirit to bring her a sea lion. The young man heard her wish. The next morning, a dead sea lion was in front of the Chief's house. All the people had a feast.

At the feast, the mother-in-law put on her dancing apron and danced and danced. She told the Food Spirit to bring her a whale.

A whale is very large. The wife was afraid that something would happen to her husband if he tried to catch a whale. But he said,

"In the morning, listen for the raven. If you hear the raven before I come back, you will know that something has happened to me. If you find me, do not let the people take me out of the skin I wear. It is the monster's skin that is bringing us the good luck. Put the monster's skin by the hollow tree beside the lake."

Again the young man put on the monster's skin and went under the sea. He had a hard time catching a whale. It took him a long time to get the whale to the shore. The whale made a great noise.

Just then the raven called. The young man was trying to get out of the monster's skin. His head was sticking out. But as the raven called, he died.

The people of the village rushed down to the shore. They saw the big whale on the shore. They thought they saw the monster with the young man's head sticking out of his mouth.

The Chief's daughter heard the raven call. She rushed down to the shore and saw her husband in the monster's skin.

"Oh, my husband, my husband," she cried.

"The monster has eaten her husband," everybody said.

But the wife said,

"My husband had killed the monster and was using his skin to get food for the people. He caught the fish, the sea lion, and the whale. For my mother is not a shaman. The Food Spirit did not send her the food. All of it was caught by my husband."

Then she told them not to take her husband's body from the skin, but to carry him, in the skin, up to the lake. There they put the body near the hollow tree.

One evening, the wife went up to the lake. She heard her husband calling, "Come to the lake and get on my back." There in the lake, she saw the monster. She got on the back of the monster. She heard her husband's voice say,

"Hold tight."

The monster swam down under the lake with his beautiful wife. They now live in the bottom of the lake and often go down the river past the village to the sea. If anyone should see the monster or his wife, good luck will come to him.

The Sad Hunter

There was a Hunter who had a wife and two little boys. He lived with his mother-in-law, as was the custom. But the mother-in-law said so many ugly things to him that he made up his mind to go away.

The Hunter kissed his wife and his two little boys. Then he said,

"Take good care of my boat and my harpoons and spears. When my sons are older, teach them how to be good hunters."

The Hunter went out on the tundra, which was a great plain without trees. He felt very sorry for himself. As he walked along, he saw some white birds. He said to himself,

"A bird is much happier than a man. I wish I were a bird."

He followed the birds. And just as he was about to speak to them, they flew over a hill.

The man walked on, trying to follow the birds. Just as the sun was going down, he walked over the hill and found a village.

As the Hunter went into the village, a man who seemed to be the Chief, said,

"Stranger, why have you followed us all day?"

Then the Hunter saw that the people in the village were the white birds turned into men.

"I want to be a white bird," said the Hunter. "A white bird is much happier than a man."

"Our life is not as happy as you think," said the Chief. "Men shoot us with bows and arrows. Animals kill us. And even other birds try to harm us."

The Hunter had not thought of the many things that could harm birds.

The bird people were very kind to the Hunter. They gave him something to eat and something to drink. When it was time to go to bed, they covered the Hunter with a white bearskin.

In the morning, when the man woke up, the village and all the bird people had gone. The man looked around. There was no white bearskin covering him. Beside him were two white feathers.

The Hunter started to walk across the tundra again. He walked and he walked and he did not care where he went.

At last he saw two rabbits playing in the grass.

"I think that I would be happy if I were a rabbit," said the

Hunter to himself. "I will follow the rabbits and perhaps they will be sorry for me. They may let me become a rabbit."

Just as the sun was going down, the rabbits went over a hill. And when the man went over the hill, he saw a lonely igloo. He went to the igloo and found an old woman and an old man eating their supper. He knew that they were the rabbits. They gave the Hunter some supper. When he had finished eating, the old man said,

"Why have you followed us all day?"

"I followed you because I thought

that you might be sorry for me," said the Hunter. "A man has nothing but trouble. If I were a rabbit, I am sure that I would be happy."

"You would not be happy if you were a rabbit," said the old man. "A rabbit has many troubles. The eagle and the hawk try to kill us. The wolves and the foxes hunt us. And even the small animals kill our babies."

The Hunter had not thought of the many things that could harm the rabbits.

The old man gave the Hunter a sleeping bag, and he went to

sleep in the igloo. In the morning, when he woke up, he was nice and warm but the sleeping bag was gone and the igloo was gone.

The Hunter started across the tundra again. He walked and he walked. At last, he saw a large herd of caribou. The caribou looked so big and fat. They were very beautiful with their big horns.

"I think that I would be happy if I were a caribou," said the Hunter to himself.

The Caribou

The Hunter wished that he could become a caribou. So he followed the herd of caribou all day. When the sun was going down, they went over a hill. When the Hunter went over the hill, he saw a large village. In the center of the village was a big kashim, or council house.

The Hunter went to the kashim and found that it was full of men. He knew that during the day, these men were caribou. They gave him food to eat and seated him in the best place, which was across from the door. When he had finished eating, the Chief said,

"Why have you followed us all day? You have no bow and arrow. You have no spear. You do not want to kill us. Why have you followed us?"

"I do not want to kill any caribou," said the Hunter. "I want to become a caribou. Then I would be happy."

"You are a man, the greatest of all animals," said the Chief. "Why do you want to become a caribou?"

Then the Hunter told the caribou

men his sad story. They all were very sorry for him.

The next morning, when the Hunter woke up, the village was gone. He looked around and saw a herd of caribou. They were kicking away the snow and eating the moss under the snow. When the Hunter looked down at his feet, he saw that he was a caribou too.

The Hunter was very happy. He ran about in the snow. And the other caribou showed him how to find the moss that was under the snow.

The Hunter lived with the caribou a long, long time. Each night, in the kashim, the Chief of the caribou told the man what would happen the next day. He did not want the Hunter to be afraid. And one night the Chief told the Hunter,

"There are two kinds of hunters. One is the black hunter. We always run away from the black hunter. The black hunter kills and kills just for his pleasure. We always know the black hunter, for we can smell his tracks in the snow. The other kind of hunter is a white hunter. The white hunter kills

only for food. Tomorrow a white
hunter will kill two caribou. But
do not be afraid, for all will be
well."

The next day, a white hunter
killed two caribou. That night two
young men came into the kashim.

"Did the white hunter skin you
in the right way?" asked the Chief.

"Yes," said one of the young
men. "He was a good white hunter
and he did everything in the right
way."

"Did the white hunter take
good care of the meat?" asked
the Chief.

"Yes," said the other young

man. "The white hunter and his wife took good care of the meat."

"We are glad to have you back with us again," said the Chief.

As the years went by, the Hunter became an old caribou. He began to think about his wife and about his two boys.

The Chief knew that the Hunter wanted to go back to his wife.

"You have been a good caribou for many years," said the Chief. "You will find it very hard to be a man again. But go back to your old home and all will be well."

The Hunter told his caribou friends goodbye and started over the tundra. When he came to where people lived, he found many snares which had been put out to catch animals. But the Hunter knew about snares and so he did not get caught.

As the Hunter got near to his home, he thought more and more about his wife and his sons. Before he knew it, he was caught in a trap. He lay very still, for he knew that he could not free himself.

Pretty soon, two young men came and they shouted for joy when they found a caribou in their trap.

"Our mother will be pleased to

have much meat," said one of the young men.

Then the caribou caught in the trap spoke to the young men very softly.

"Please take off my skin very carefully," said the caribou.

The young men were so surprised that they could not move. The caribou spoke very softly and said again,

"Please take off my skin very carefully."

The young men got their sharp knives and took the skin off the caribou very carefully. They saw that there was a man inside the caribou skin.

The man went home with the two young men. There he found his dear wife who had waited for him all these years. The two young men were his sons who had grown up. The mother-in-law had been dead many years.

The Hunter was now an old man. He was glad to be with his family again. But when he walked, he was bent over, for he had walked like a caribou for so many, many years.

Raven and Fox

Raven thought that he was very smart. He thought that he was smarter than anyone else. But Fox thought that he was smart too. He thought that he was the smartest animal in the world.

Raven did not like Fox. And Fox did not like Raven. But each was very polite to the other. You would have thought that they were the best of friends.

One day Raven thought of a way that he could get the best of Fox. He went to Fox and said,

"Friend Fox, won't you come and play with me? Let us play slide-down-the-hill. We will have a lot of fun."

Now Fox did not want Raven to know that he did not want to play with him. For then Raven might think that Fox was afraid of him. So Fox said,

"Friend Raven, I would like to play slide-down-the-hill with you."

Raven laughed to himself. He knew the hill that he wanted to slide on. And he knew that at the bottom was a pond of mud.

Fox knew about the hill too. And he knew that at the bottom

of the hill was the pond of mud. But he did not say anything.

Fox and Raven climbed to the top of the hill.

"You thought of the game," said Fox. "You should be the first to slide down the hill."

"Very well," said Raven. "You watch carefully and see how I slide down the hill."

Down the hill went Raven. He went down the hill so fast that when he came to the bottom, he could not stop. But he did not need to. He just spread his wings and he flew right over the pond of mud at the bottom of the hill.

Then Raven called to Fox.

"It is your turn now. Let me see how well you can slide."

"Oh, no," said Fox. "I know that there is a pond of mud at the bottom of the hill. I will fall right into it."

"Can't you jump over the pond of mud just as well as I did?" said Raven. "Come. Show how you can slide down the hill."

Fox knew that he would have to slide down the hill just to show that he was as smart as Raven. And he thought that if Raven had jumped over the pond of mud, he could jump over it too.

So Fox started sliding down the hill. Faster and faster he went. When he came near the bottom, he saw the pond of mud. He gave a great big jump. And the jump landed him right in the middle of the pond of mud.

Raven laughed and laughed.

Poor Fox dragged himself out of the pond of mud. And he looked so funny that Raven laughed some more.

Fox ran away to his igloo to hide. And from that time, Fox and Raven were never friends again.

Keok and Maleyat

Keok and Maleyat were friends. Keok lived on the seashore. He caught seals and sometimes he caught a big black whale. The people of the village came to his igloo and he gave them meat to eat. But the skins of the seals and the oil of the whales he kept.

When the winter came and ice and snow was over all the land, Keok would load his sled with the skins and the oil. He would hitch his dogs to the sled. Then Keok would drive across the tundra to where his friend, Maleyat, lived.

Maleyat was a great hunter. He killed many caribou. The people of his village came to his igloo and he gave them much meat. But the skins of the caribou he kept for himself. These caribou skins he traded with his friend, Keok, for the seal skins and the whale oil.

One day Maleyat's mother and father said to him,

"It is time you married, for we want to see your children before we die."

Maleyat wanted to please his father and his mother. So he said to the girls of the village,

"Come to my igloo and I will give each one of you a caribou skin. You can make yourself a beautiful parka. And I will marry the girl whose needle makes no noise when she sews her parka."

All of the girls came to Maleyat's igloo and he gave each one a caribou skin. And such a noise you never heard. For, try as they would, there was not one girl that could sew without making a noise with her needle. The girls talked all the time. And most of their talk was about a poor girl who lived at the end of the village.

Maleyat heard the girls talking.

He wondered why the poor girl who lived with her grandmother had not come to make a parka.

Maleyat took one of his most beautiful caribou skins. He went to the little igloo at the edge of the village. There he found a beautiful girl living with her grandmother.

"Would you like to make yourself a parka of the caribou skin?" asked Maleyat.

"Oh, yes," said the girl, for she had never had a beautiful parka.

When the girl sewed her parka, you could not hear her needle.

Maleyat said to the grandmother,

"I wish to marry your grand-daughter."

The grandmother was very pleased. The beautiful girl was pleased too, for she loved Maleyat.

Maleyat was very happy. His wife cooked his meat over the fire. She kept his igloo clean.

But one day, Maleyat got a message from Keok's mother and father. Keok had gone out on the ice to hunt seal. And he had not come home.

Maleyat loved his friend very much. He went at once to the village where Keok lived. The men of the village all shook their heads. But Maleyat went out over the ice and snow. At last he found the tracks of Keok's snowshoes.

Soon Maleyat heard someone crying, "Let me go. Let me go."

Maleyat climbed a hill of snow and ice and looked around. He saw a small tent almost hidden by a pile of ice. He rushed to the tent. In it were two strangers trying to kill Keok. Maleyat killed the strangers with his spear.

The two friends went back to the village.

"My friend," said Keok, "you have saved my life."

Maleyat went back to his village. It was not long before he went out on the tundra hunting caribou. And he did not return. The men of the village went out on the tundra. But they could not find Maleyat.

It was then that Maleyat's father sent a message to Keok. Keok came at once. He went out to look for Maleyat.

There was no snow on the tundra at that time of year. But Keok soon found Maleyat's tracks in the grass. He found where Maleyat had killed a caribou. Then Maleyat's tracks stopped.

Keok could not tell what had happened. He sat down on the tundra and tried to think.

All at once, Keok saw some grass begin to move. He looked very hard at the grass, and he suddenly saw a door open in the ground. He knew that this must be a magic door. A big brown bear came out of the door.

Keok rushed at the bear and killed it with his spear. Then he went through the door. He found Maleyat and pulled him out just as the door began to close.

"You have saved my life," said Maleyat.

"It was in return for my life," said Keok. "If you had not come, the strangers would have killed me."

The two friends went back to the village. There was feasting and dancing. And then Keok went back to his own village by the seashore.

Keok became the Chief of his village. And Maleyat became the Chief of his village. The two friends lived to be old, old men.

The Starving Time

There was an orphan boy whose name was Puzwuk. He had no home, for he had no father and he had no mother.

When Puzwuk was a little boy, he lived first in one house and then in another. A family would let him live with them for a while. But sooner or later, they would ask him to find another place to live.

Puzwuk was lonely, for he had no one to love. At last, a woman of the village who had lost her husband let the boy live in her house. Puzwuk tried in every way to be good to this kind woman. And he lived for a long time in this home.

As Puzwuk grew older, he tried in every way to grow big and strong. Every morning he ran down the beach as fast as he could. And every morning he tried to run a little longer and a little faster. Before long Puzwuk was the best runner in the village.

Then the starving time came.

A great wind blew the ice up on the beach. The hunters could catch no seals. There were no fish and no birds. The polar bears did not come down from the north. The hunters could find nothing for the people of the village to eat. It was the starving time.

Soon the food in the igloos was almost gone. There was very little oil left for the seal oil lamps that kept the igloos warm. The people all went to the kashim or council house. They put their furs around them to keep them warm. Only a few seal oil lamps were burning in the kashim. What little food there was left was carefully divided among the people. They were all very, very hungry.

The woman who had been good

to Puzwuk had a little dry fish left. Puzwuk had fished every day until the fish had gone away. The woman had carefully dried the fish he had caught. Now, every day the woman took a dried fish and divided it among the people in the kashim. It was just a little bite for each one, but it kept the people alive.

Every day Puzwuk went out of the kashim to see if he could find anything for the people to eat. The other men stayed in the kashim and tried to keep warm. They knew that soon there would be no more food. And soon there would be no more oil for the seal oil lamps. Then they would sit in the darkness and freeze to death.

But Puzwuk would not give up. Every day he ran up and down the beach that was covered with snow and ice. One day he saw three small birds, the first living things he had seen for many days. He ran after the birds. Because he was such a fast runner he caught one of the birds. He took it to the kashim.

The people said, "Look. The boy we put out of our homes has caught a little bird. And he brings it to us in the starving time."

Puzwuk gave the little bird to the woman who had been good to him. And she divided it among the people in the kashim.

The next day, Puzwuk went out on the snow and ice. He caught a bigger bird. And the bigger bird was divided among the people in the kashim.

The people said, "Look. The boy we put out of our homes has caught a bigger bird. And he brings it to us in the starving time. We are sorry we put him out of our homes."

By now there was only one seal oil lamp burning, and it was very dark in the kashim. Soon the cold would come in and the people would freeze to death.

The next day, Puzwuk climbed a hill of snow and looked out over the sea. Far out over the ice he could see some dark holes. And he knew they were openings where he might find a seal. The seal would put his head up out of the water to get air.

When Puzwuk woke up in the morning, the kashim was dark. The last seal oil lamp had gone out. It was very still.

"I will catch a seal today," said Puzwuk to himself.

Puzwuk took a harpoon and a spear and went out over the ice. It took him a long time to get to the seal holes.

At last Puzwuk got to a hole in the ice where a seal must come up to get air. He held his harpoon ready. He waited by that seal hole for a very long time.

Then suddenly a brown head came out of the open water. Puzwuk drove the harpoon into the seal.

The seal was very heavy, but Puzwuk got it out of the hole and onto the ice. At last

Puzwuk got the seal back to the kashim.

"I have brought you a seal," Puzwuk cried to the starving people. The woman cut up the seal. Puzwuk put new seal oil into the lamps.

The woman gave each one seal meat to eat. They all became warm and more alive.

The Polar Bear

The wind had driven the ice up on the beach. The seals had gone. The birds had gone. The fish had gone. The people of the village were sitting in the council house or kashim, waiting to die.

Puzwuk had gone out and caught a little bird for the people. He had caught a large bird for the people. He had even caught a seal for them. They were still alive, and the seal oil lamps were still burning to keep the kashim warm.

But this was not enough. The starving time was not over. All the people would die unless Puzwuk could find more food for them.

The next morning, Puzwuk took his harpoon and his spear. He went out of the kashim. He started to go over the ice to the hole where he had found the seal.

As he went over the ice, a snow storm came. The wind blew. And there was so much snow that Puzwuk did not know where he was going.

Puzwuk did not want to go back to the kashim without any food for the people. So he slowly went on in the snow. Soon he lost his way. He found himself on the side of a large hill made up of piles of ice pushed up by the wind.

Suddenly Puzwuk heard a great roar. He thought that the hill of ice had broken off from the shore and would go out to sea. Then he heard the roar again. This time it seemed closer to him. He stood still and looked all around. The snowing had stopped.

Then Puzwuk saw, coming over the ice and snow, the biggest polar bear he had ever seen.

Now Puzwuk knew that this was starving time for the polar bears as well as for his people. This polar bear must be very hungry. So the bear wanted to catch an Eskimo just as he would catch a rabbit or a seal.

Puzwuk was a fast runner. He started to run around the hill of ice and snow. The polar bear ran after him. The boy went around and around the hill. The polar bear was right behind him.

Little by little, Puzwuk got ahead of the polar bear. Soon the bear could not see him but the bear was following his tracks in the snow. Then Puzwuk slipped and fell. As he did so, he saw a hole in the cakes of ice. Quickly, he hid himself in the hole.

The polar bear did not know that the boy had hidden himself. So he raced around and around the hill of ice. Puzwuk could hear him roar as he went by his hiding place.

Puzwuk said to himself,

"The next time that bear passes by, I shall throw my spear. I shall hit the bear in the heart and kill him. Then there will be much food for the people."

Puzwuk got his spear ready. He knew he must hit the bear's heart, or he could not kill him with a spear. Soon he heard the roar of the polar bear. And just

as the polar bear passed by, Puzwuk
threw the spear and hit the bear
in the heart.

With a last roar, the bear fell
in the snow. Puzwuk had killed
him.

The bear was so big that Puzwuk
could not move him. As the snow
was not falling, Puzwuk could see
where he was. So he started out
to the village. It was a hard
journey, for the snow was deep,
but Puzwuk at last got to the
kashim.

The woman who had been good
to him was so glad to see him.
She had been afraid he was lost.

"I have killed a polar bear," said Puzwuk. "There will be plenty of food for all the people. But all the men who are strong enough must come with me to bring the bear in."

All the people in the kashim said,

"Look. The boy we put out of our homes when he was little has killed a polar bear. We are sorry we were not kind to him. Now he will give meat to all of us. The starving time is over."

The Shaman

In a village there was a shaman,
or witch doctor. He could do great
magic. The shaman had four
brothers and one sister, who was
very beautiful. They all lived with
their mother in an igloo.

One night there was a very bad
storm. The wind blew the snow
around the igloo. Then one of the
boys asked his mother for something to eat.

"There is no water," said the
mother. "I cannot boil the meat."

"I will get some water for you,"
said the sister.

The girl and the youngest brother went down to the water hole in the ice. Just as they had filled the tub with water, the wind, blowing from the land, blew the shore ice out to sea.

In the morning, the four brothers went down to the shore to hunt for their sister and their brother. They saw the dark water where the ice had been. The shaman knew that the wind had blown the ice out to sea with his sister and his brother.

The shaman was very sad, for he loved his beautiful sister. All winter long he made great magic.

At last his spirit came and told him that his sister had landed on an island far away. His youngest brother had been drowned.

When spring came, the shaman and his brothers made a big skin boat called a umiak. When it was ready, the shaman told their mother to put food into the boat and an old coat made of bird's skin. Then the shaman and his three brothers started for the island far away.

After many days, the brothers came to the far away island. They stopped at a village.

The Chief of the village and all his men were in the kashim or council house. The shaman and his brothers asked for their sister. But the men of the village rushed at the strangers and were going to kill them.

The shaman closed both his eyes. He made a great magic. Every man shut his eyes and no man could open them.

The Chief of the village and all his men were very much afraid.

"Where is my sister?" asked the shaman.

"She is not here," said the Chief. "She may be at the next

village. But be careful, for a very wicked shaman lives there."

The shaman opened his eyes. Then the Chief and all his men could open their eyes.

The shaman and his three brothers got into their umiak. After four days, they came to the second village. They did not go up to the village but stopped on the shore. Then the shaman put on the old birdskin coat that his mother had put into the umiak. He bent his body, and he looked like an old, old man.

"Carry me up to the kashim," said the shaman to his brothers.

"Put me in a corner of the kashim and then ask the Chief of the village where your sister is."

When the brothers got to the kashim, the men said,

"Why do you carry such an old man about?"

"He is no trouble at all," said one of the brothers.

"Why have you come to our village?" asked the Chief.

"We are looking for our sister. The wind blew her out to sea on the ice."

"Yes," said the Chief of the village. "Your sister is here. She is the wife of the shaman of our

village. She is very happy and
wants to stay with us."

The Chief had a feast for the
strangers. There was beating of
drums and dancing. The shaman
showed the strangers his beautiful
wife. She was dressed in rich furs
and the brothers could hardly see
her face.

But that night, one of the
brothers went to the shaman's
house. He heard someone crying
in a shed beside the house. He
crawled into the shed and found
his sister lying on the floor. Her
hands and her feet were tied. He
quickly untied her.

"My dear sister, these wicked people have almost killed you," he said.

"My dear brother, I am so glad that you have found me," said the sister. "It is the shaman who has treated me so badly. He has given me hardly anything to eat."

"Stay here and be quiet," said the brother. "I will come back for you."

The brother went back to the kashim. He went to the corner where the brother, who was a shaman, seemed to be asleep. He told him how he had found his sister.

The wicked shaman of the village saw the two talking together. He took his spear and was going to kill them. But the shaman brother threw off his old birdskin coat and stood up. He took hold of the wicked shaman and threw him to the ground and killed him.

The people of the village were happy that the wicked shaman was dead. He had been a bad man and had hurt many people.

The Chief of the village gave the four brothers and their sister a fine igloo to live in. They lived in the village many days.

The Return

The shaman and his three
brothers stayed on the far away
island a long time. But one day
the shaman said,

"Our mother will be looking for
us. Let us go to our own village."

The shaman made great magic
to find out if the return home was
to be a good journey. But he
could not find out. So he went to
an old woman in the village.

"Go to your spirits," he said,
"and find out if our return is to
be a good journey."

The old woman went to sleep, and when she woke she told the shaman,

"You will have a good journey. But great harm will come to you unless you do just as I tell you. Make ready for the trip, and then I will tell you what you must do."

The shaman and his brothers got the umiak, or skin boat, ready for the trip. The Chief of the village gave them much food and many fine furs to take home.

At last all was ready. Then the old woman came down to the sea. She was carrying a stone dish. In the dish, a fire was burning.

"Take this fire with you," said the old woman to the shaman. "Keep it burning. And when you get to the seashore in front of your village, make a big pile of the wood that is on the seashore. Light the wood from this fire that I am giving you. Do this the very first thing. Then all will be well."

The shaman and his brothers paddled for many days across the sea. The sister kept the fire burning in the stone dish. At last they saw their village.

When they got to the land, the shaman jumped out of the boat to pull it closer into the shore.

"Be careful," called the sister. "Remember what the old woman told you. Make a pile of wood and light it with this fire."

But the shaman did not hear his sister. He ran along the beach, pulling the boat through the water with a rope made of seal hide. He was so happy that he did not remember what the old woman had told him about the fire.

All of a sudden, the shaman stopped. He stood very still. He had turned into stone. The seal hide rope behind him turned into stone. And the umiak in the water, and his three brothers and his sister in it, turned into stone.

To this day, on the seashore in front of the village, you can see the stone man, who had forgotten to do what he had been told to do. You can still see the stone rope behind him. And in the water close to the shore, you can see the stone boat. In the boat are the three brothers and the beautiful sister, all turned to stone. They are all looking toward the village, to which they never returned.

How to Say Some
Alaskan Words

Words divided into syllables	How to say the word
car-i-bou	kar-i-boo
ig-loo	ig-loo
kash-im	kash-im
Ke-ok	Kee-ok
Ma-le-yat	Mah-lay-yat
par-ka	par-kuh
pot-latch	pot-latch
Puz-wuk	Puz-wuk
sha-man	shaw-man
tun-dra	tun-druh
u-mi-ak	oo-mi-ak